Hello, Family Members,

Learning to read is one of the most important accomplishments of early childhood. **Hello Reader!** books are designed to help children become skilled readers who like to read. Beginning readers learn to read by remembering frequently used words like "the," "is," and "and"; by using phonics skills to decode new words; and by interpreting picture and text clues. These books provide both the stories children enjoy and the structure they need to read fluently and independently. Here are suggestions for helping your child *before*, *during*, and *after* reading:

Before

- Look at the cover and pictures and have your child predict what the story is about.
- Read the story to your child.
- Encourage your child to chime in with familiar words and phrases.
- Echo read with your child by reading a line first and having your child read it after you do.

During

- Have your child think about a word he or she does not recognize right away. Provide hints such as "Let's see if we know the sounds" and "Have we read other words like this one?"
- Encourage your child to use phonics skills to sound out new words.
- Provide the word for your child when more assistance is needed so that he or she does not struggle and the experience of reading with you is a positive one.
- Encourage your child to have fun by reading with a lot of expression . . . like an actor!

After

- Have your child keep lists of interesting and favorite words.
- Encourage your child to read the books over and over again. Have him or her read to brothers, sisters, grandparents, and even teddy bears. Repeated readings develop confidence in young readers.
- Talk about the stories. Ask and answer questions. Share ideas about the funniest and most interesting characters and events in the stories.

I do hope that you and your child enjoy this book.

—Francie Alexander
Reading Specialist,
Scholastic's Instructional Publishing Group

To Timothy and Michael McNulty,
with love
— F.M.

T 578

Text copyright © 1998 by Faith McNulty.
Illustrations copyright © 1998 by Lena Shiffman.
All rights reserved. Published by Scholastic Inc.
SCHOLASTIC, HELLO READER!, CARTWHEEL BOOKS and associated logos
are trademarks and/or registered trademarks of Scholastic Inc.

Library of Congress Cataloging-in-Publication Data

McNulty, Faith.
    When I lived with bats / by Faith McNulty; illustrated by Lena Shiffman.
       p.   cm.—(Hello reader! Science. Level 4)
    Summary: A girl describes how she spent a summer observing the bats around and inside her house and what she discovered about their characteristics and behavior.
    ISBN 0-590-04980-1
    1. Bats—Juvenile literature. [1. Bats.] I. Shiffman, Lena, ill.
II. Title. III. Series.
QL737.C5M425   1998
599.4—dc21
                                                     98-6548
                                                        CIP
                                                        AC

12 11 10 9 8 7 6 5 4 3   9/9 0/0 01 02 03

Printed in the U.S.A.   23
First printing, September 1998

When I Lived With Bats

by Faith McNulty
Illustrated by Lena Shiffman

Hello Reader! Science —Level 4

SCHOLASTIC INC.
New York   Toronto   London   Auckland   Sydney

Bats are weird.
Bats are scary.
They hate the sun
and love the night.

Bats can see in the dark.
They get in your hair.
Bats are dangerous and bad.

None of this is true,
but this is what I believed
until the summer that I lived
with bats.

My family had rented
an old farmhouse.
I was about ten
and my brother was twelve.
We look back on it as our "Bat Summer."

In the evening,
while the sky was still pale gray,
we would see dark wings
flitting over the yard.
At first, I thought
they were some sort of night bird.
Mom said no. They were bats
catching mosquitoes in the air.
She said bats sleep in the daytime
so they can hunt at night
when there are lots of insects
and no birds to compete with.

Of course, I had seen pictures of bats.
They looked like mice with wings.
In pictures, they were black and ugly.
I believed bats were vampires
and drank your blood.
Mom said, "Don't worry. That's not true."
Watching them dip and swoop
over the yard,
I decided I wouldn't go out after sunset
in case a bat might swoop into my hair.

I got used to seeing bats
flying over the yard.
Then we found that
bats were not just outdoors.
They were in the house, too.

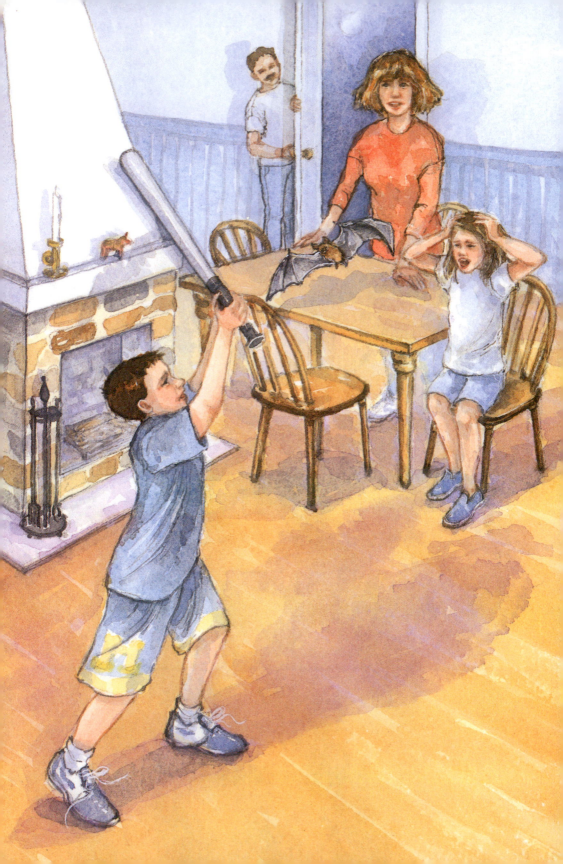

We were sitting in the kitchen
in the late afternoon.
There was a noise in the chimney.
Dust fell into the fireplace.
In another instant, a bat was
swooping around the room.
Mom and Dad jumped up
out of their chairs.
I shrieked.
My brother yelled, "I'll get him!"
He picked up a baseball bat
and began waving it.

Mom said, "No! Don't hurt it!"
The bat flitted around the room,
always out of reach.
Dad opened the kitchen door wide
and stood back.
The bat swooped out and
disappeared into the evening sky.

"They must be living in the chimney,"
Mom said. "I'm glad we didn't light a fire."

My brother said, "Mom, why wouldn't you
let me kill it? Do you want bats in the house?"

"I don't *want* them in the house," she said.
"But I don't want you to kill anything
unless you absolutely have to.
The bat wasn't doing any harm."

The next bat was in my parents' bedroom.
They found it when they went
up to bed. I heard their voices
and ran into the room. "There it is."
Mom pointed at a window.
Her voice was calm.
The bat was hanging
from the top of a curtain.
Dad went toward it and the
bat swiftly flew around the room.
When it came in my direction, I was scared,
but it made a quick turn and swooped away.
"Don't worry," Dad said. "The last thing
that bat wants is to get tangled in your hair.
It just wants to get out of here."

I could see the bat's beating wings,
its pointed ears and open mouth.
It flitted close to the ceiling and walls,
but never touched them.

"It's using its radar," Dad said.
He opened a window at the top.
In an instant, the bat was gone.

He explained that when they fly,
bats open their mouths and
make tiny squeaks — too shrill for us to hear.
When the sound waves hit something solid,
they bounce back. This echo tells the bat
the location of any object,
even one as small as a mosquito.
It's called *echolocation*.
Bats use their eyes in the daytime,
and echolocation to hunt at night.

In the morning, Mom and Dad
discussed the bat problem.
How did it get in the bedroom?
Were bats living in the house?
What should we do about it?
Nobody knew the answers.

A few days later, I saw a bat up close
for the first time.
It was hanging from a picture frame
in the living room.
I called Mom. She came in
and opened a window,
but the bat didn't fly.

We moved closer to it. It was hanging
head down, its hind toes hooked on the frame,
its wings partly folded. In the air, bats look big.
Now I could see that this one was really small —
about the size of a mouse. It had brown fur,
except on its wings. They were hairless
and paper-thin.

The bat looked up at us with small,
shiny black eyes.
Its face was round and its ears pointed,
like a cat's ears. When Mom came near,
it made tiny squeaking sounds.

Still the bat didn't fly.
Mom said maybe it had flown
around the room until it was too tired.
She went to the kitchen
and came back with a plastic container.
She covered the bat with it,
slid the lid onto it,
and carried the bat out to the yard.

"I think it needs a perch," she said.
"Bats have trouble taking off from the ground."
She went to an open shed and shook the bat
out of the container onto a high shelf.
We watched from a distance as the bat
pulled itself together, stretched out its wings,
then launched into the air.
It zoomed over our heads and disappeared
into the branches of a tree.

The next bat caused a lot more commotion.
When Aunt Sue came to visit, we didn't
tell her about the bats; we didn't want to
spook her.

After supper, Aunt Sue said
she would love a good hot bath.
She went upstairs;
we heard her running the water.

Five minutes later, we heard a shriek
and dashed upstairs.
Mom went into the bathroom.
Behind the closed door, I could hear her saying,
"Sue! It's only a bat! Calm down!
No, you are not dreaming.
Yes, there *is* a bat in the tub!
It won't hurt you!"

Aunt Sue stopped shrieking
and Mom came out with a washcloth
in which she had caught the bat.
She was trying to stifle her laughter.

It seems the bat must have been
hanging from the shower curtain
while Aunt Sue was relaxing in the tub.
She gave the curtain a push,
and the bat fell into the water.

When Mom arrived, the bat was swimming,
and Aunt Sue was trying to hide underwater.
After Mom fished the bat out,
she took it to the shed.
Even though it was pretty soggy,
it managed to fly.

Aunt Sue is a sport.
The next day she went to
the library with Mom and
they brought home bat books.

Bats are mouselike animals,
but they are not mice.
Nor are they related to birds.

Birds probably came from reptiles that
lived in the age of dinosaurs.
Bats belong to a group of animals called
mammals.
It includes all the different kinds of animals
from mice to elephants that give birth to live
young and feed them with milk.
Human beings belong to that group, too.

Bats are very much like other mammals
except for one extraordinary difference.
They are the only mammal that can fly.

We can guess that millions of years ago,
a small, furry animal climbed trees to hunt insects.
Perhaps it began to glide from tree to tree
with front and hind legs outstretched.

Little by little, the skin of its back and belly
stretched enough to cover the space
between its front legs and hind legs.
Finally, this flap of skin became a wing.

Hold out your arms.
Imagine that your fingers are growing
until they are as long as your
forearms.
Imagine that your legs are spread
apart, and that you have a tail.
Imagine skin attached to your body
and stretched from the tip of your tail
to your ankles and fingers
and then to your shoulders;
that's what a bat's wing is like.

Fruit Bats

Bats live in every part of the world
and, of all wildlife, they are the most gentle
and harmless.
There are many species of bats,
but only one — the vampire bat —
will deliberately
bite a human.

Vampire Bat

Most species of bats live in caves or hollow trees,
but one species, the little brown bat,
likes the warmth and safety of buildings.

In the spring, females roost together to have
their babies.
At night, while the mothers hunt,
the baby bats cling together to keep warm.
They play together, too.

Big-Eared Bat

There are no vampire bats in North America,
or any kind of bat that will attack a person.
Some people fear that bats carry disease.
This is rarely, if ever, a problem.
However, the books warned against picking up
a sick bat.
There is a chance — about one in a thousand —
that it has rabies, a very serious disease.
Bats, like all wild animals, should be handled
with care.

In the autumn, when the young bats can fly,
the colony leaves for a winter home.

Bats living in an attic or under the eaves are
usually no bother to the people in the house.
Even so, some people want to get rid of them.
To do this in summer is cruel. If mother bats
are killed, or shut out of the nursery, their
babies die of starvation.

The books urged people who find bats living in the house to let them stay until the young bats are able to fly, when they will all leave of their own accord.

After they are gone, it is okay to close up all the entrances to prevent them from returning in the spring.

Mom and Dad agreed that the bats were welcome to spend the summer with us.

"They're probably in the attic, coming in and going out through some little hole we haven't noticed," Mom said.
"If one comes down here by mistake, it's easy enough to shoo it out.
Just don't handle one with your bare hands."

"Can I go look for them?" my brother asked.
When Mom said no, he sulked.

One afternoon, my brother told me
he was going to hunt for bats.
I asked, "What for?"
He said, "Just because."

I knew it was a bad idea, but I followed him.
He was carrying a flashlight and a
tennis racquet.
Someone had told him that a bat can't
echolocate a tennis racquet in the dark
because of the holes.

We climbed steep stairs.
My brother pushed open the attic door.
It was dark inside — warm and musty.
My brother shone the beam of the flashlight
on the eaves.

"There!" my brother shouted.
In a corner where rafters met,
I saw a cluster of dark shapes
hanging like tiny umbrellas.
He moved closer. He reached up
with the racquet and touched a bat.
In an instant, it was flying around.
Then there were dozens in the air.

I ran for the door, but my brother
was swinging the tennis racquet.
"Don't!" I yelled just as the racquet knocked a
bat to the floor.

The bat flopped on the floor.
I knew it was hurt.

My brother picked it up. We both ran.
Once outside, my brother opened his hands.
The bat crouched down.
It looked small and afraid.

Then I saw there was blood on one wing.
Suddenly I felt awful.

Just then Mom arrived.
She was very upset
that the bat had been hurt.
She told my brother to put it in a box
with breathing holes
so we could take it to the vet.

When we got there,
the vet was nice about it.
He said he would do his best
to fix the bat's broken wing.
When it got better,
we could take it back home.
He also said that the bat had been
nursing a baby; it was too bad,
but the baby would die
before we could bring the mother back.

My brother looked shocked.
I knew that he felt sorry and ashamed.

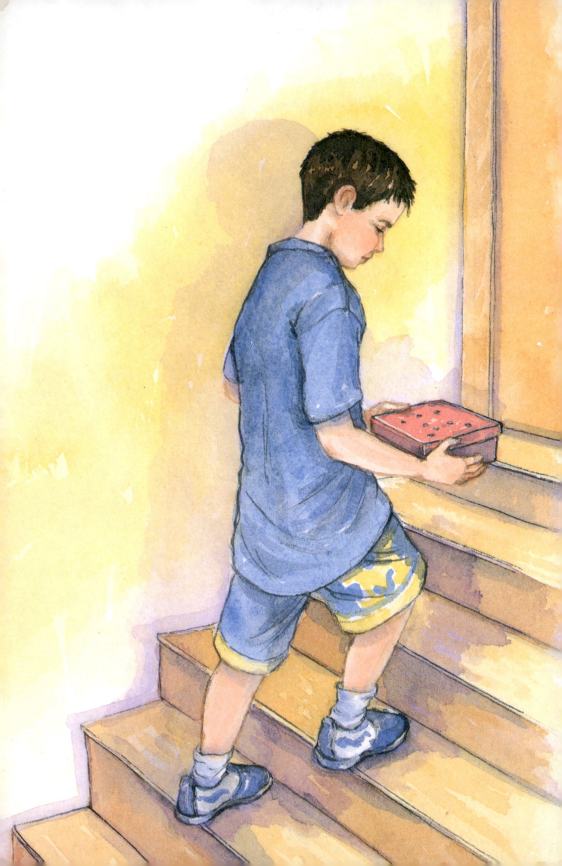

A few weeks later, we brought
the bat home from the hospital.
In the evening, when the mother bats
were out hunting,
my brother carried the box up to the attic.
I followed and watched
as he gently slid the bat onto a low beam.
For a moment it huddled there,
then spread its wings
and disappeared into the darkness.

As we went down the stairs, I saw
that my brother was smiling.
I knew he'd been sorry about the harm
that he'd done and felt better now.

Later, when the sun set, we went
outdoors and waited for the bats
to come out.

I saw one, then another, swoop through
the twilight sky, like
figure skaters on ice.
I thought of how small they were; how fragile
and easily hurt, with only wings and a tiny brain
to depend on. I wondered how I could ever have
been afraid of them.
After that, my brother, too, was changed.

He became interested in learning about animals
and never wanted to hurt one again.